LEONARDO RETURNS

by Jake Black
based on the screenplay by Kevin Munroe
illustrated by Diego Jourdan

Ready-to-Read

SIMON SPOTLIGHT
New York   London   Toronto   Sydney

Based on the film *TMNT*™ by Imagi Animation Studios and Warner Bros.

SIMON SPOTLIGHT
An imprint of Simon & Schuster Children's Publishing Division
1230 Avenue of the Americas, New York, New York 10020
© 2007 Mirage Studios, Inc. *Teenage Mutant Ninja Turtles*™ and *TMNT*™
are trademarks of Mirage Studios, Inc. All rights reserved.
SIMON SPOTLIGHT, READY-TO-READ, and colophon are registered trademarks
of Simon & Schuster, Inc. All rights reserved, including the right of reproduction in
whole or in part in any form.
Manufactured in the United States of America
First Edition
2 4 6 8 10 9 7 5 3 1
Cataloging-in-Publication Data for this book is available from the Library of Congress.
ISBN-13: 978-1-4169-4056-2
ISBN-10: 1-4169-4056-1

CHAPTER ONE

I had been gone for a long time.

I was sent to finish my ninja training in the jungle.

Now I'm back to train my brothers, the Teenage Mutant Ninja Turtles.

My name is Leonardo. I am their leader.

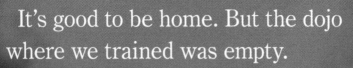

It's good to be home. But the dojo where we trained was empty.

"Doesn't ANYBODY train anymore?" I yelled.

Michelangelo looked up from his video game. "Just a sec, dude! I'm almost at level eighteen!"

"Donny!" I called out. Donatello was in his lab.

"In a few minutes, Leo. I'm in the middle of—"

KZZZT-BOOM! An explosion shook the dojo.

"Uh, I'll be there in an hour," Donatello said.

"A true leader knows how to motivate his troops," Master Splinter told me.

What he said gave me an idea. I turned off the power in the dojo, and everything went out.

"Ninja tag, topside!" I yelled.

It was time to train.

CHAPTER TWO

A minute later Michelangelo, Donatello, Raphael, and I were on the roof. There was a large billboard not too far away.

"First one to touch old faithful over there—" Michelangelo began.

". . . does the other team's chores for a week," Donatello finished.

"Deal," Raphael and I said together.

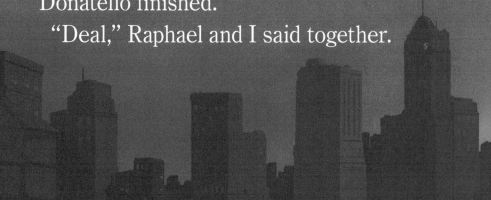

Raphael and I hadn't really spoken to each other since I got home. I could tell something was bothering him. Maybe training together would help us patch things up.

Running across the rooftops required teamwork. I accidentally shoved Raphael into a wall. He thought I did it on purpose!

"Are you trying to make me mad?" Raph asked.

In return Raphael threw me hard over the billboard—too hard! I couldn't touch it and we lost the game.

"I understand you're upset," I said.

"You wouldn't understand the first thing about me, daddy's boy!" Raphael yelled.

"Is that what this is about? You think Splinter likes me best?" I asked.

Raphael turned his shell to me. "Isn't that the truth?" he replied coldly.

Before I could answer, Michelangelo said, "So nice of you to join us, gentledudes," as he and Donatello high-fived each other.

CHAPTER THREE

It was a long, slow walk across the rooftops back to the dojo. Raphael didn't say much, and I didn't either.

Suddenly Michelangelo broke the silence. "Whoa! What's that?" he asked, pointing to a building under construction. "You dudes see those shadows over there?"

We all saw the large shadows at the construction site. It was dangerous to be that high up on a building that wasn't finished yet.

"So, what now, Captain?" Michelangelo asked me.

"We need to come up with a plan," I said.

Raphael didn't want to wait. "Later!" he said as he ran toward the construction site.

"Raph!" I called out, but he ignored me.

"Welcome home, bro," Michelangelo said.

It didn't take long for us to catch up with Raphael. We crossed over to the building and started to scale up the wall, heading for the top floor.

Donatello pointed to the deep claw
marks in some of the I beams that made up
the building's frame.

"Guys, I've got a bad feeling—," he said.

"Come on, let's take a peek," Raphael said.

The four of us made our way to the top floor. We looked down over the edge and saw who was making the shadows.

"The good news is," Michelangelo said, "that there are a bunch of Foot Ninjas getting beaten up. The bad news is *what's* beating them up."

CHAPTER FOUR

Michelangelo was right. A giant werewolf was tossing the Foot around like stuffed animals.

"Well, what do we do now?" Donatello asked. "Do we help the Foot?"

"Let's sit back and watch the show," Michelangelo said. "What do you say, leader boy?"

I wasn't sure. But once again Raphael made a quick decision.

"I say we go for it!" he said, before jumping down to join the Foot and the monster.

We quickly followed Raphael, and the four of us surprised the werewolf and the Foot.

The leader of the Foot drew her katana as she stepped forward.

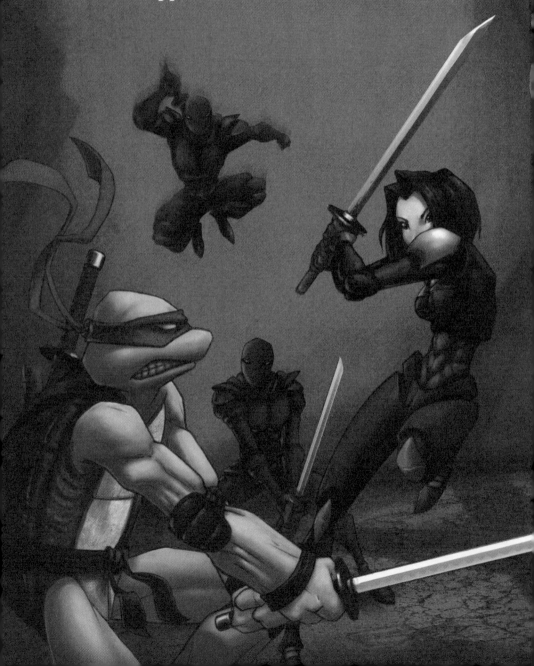

"Who are you?" I asked.

But she didn't answer. Instead she came toward me swinging her sword!

My brothers attacked the creature, using all of their ninja skills.

The Foot leader swung at me, knocking me to the floor. I leaped to my feet, but she was gone. The other Foot had escaped as well, leaving us to fight the monster!

I charged at the creature, but just as I did it threw my brothers into the air. Raph fell off the side of the building but was able to swing to safety. Michelangelo and Donatello landed on the ground.

23

The monster slammed its fist into the floor, shattering the ground beneath us. We crashed onto the same floor that Raphael had landed on.

"Nice of you to join me," he said.
Michelangelo spun his nunchakus
and screamed out, "Yeeeaaaargghh!"

With a mighty roar, the creature
howled as it punched an I beam.
The blow shook the building, and
suddenly a large stack of cement blocks
landed on top of us! We tried to dig
our way out of the rubble.

"Get me out of here!" Mikey said.

"Working on it," I said, using my katana
to dig through the blocks.

Just then there was a blinding flash of light, then a loud *BOOM!* as the ground shook.

I shoved the last few cement blocks out of the way, and we were finally free.

My brothers and I climbed out and looked around at all the rubble.

"Where's the monster?" Raphael asked.

It had left. The only sounds we heard were police sirens.

"Better hit the tunnels," Donatello said, heading for a manhole cover. We couldn't have agreed more.

CHAPTER FIVE

It had been a very strange night. We had set out to train, but wound up fighting a monster and the Foot—under cement blocks!

"Did anyone get the license plate of the monster that hit us?" Mikey asked.

"We could have finished it if it hadn't disappeared," said Raphael. He patted me on the shell and smiled. "And that woman sure gave you a run for your money, bro."

I looked at Raphael. We hadn't patched things up, but this was a start.

We may not have defeated the monster, but we will fight another day—the four of us, together.

And whatever happens, it *is* good to be home.